GIVE A DOG A BONE

MICHAEL KINGSWOOD

Contents

About This Book

While on a run through a park with his best buddy John, Harry the dog makes a grim discovery in the woods.

Give A Dog A Bone is a 3,200 word doggy mystery.

Enjoy the book! After you're done, please come to Michael's website and sign up for his mailing list at michaelkingswood.com/newsletter-signup/. Guaranteed to be spam free, he uses it to announce new releases and special promotions for his fans.

Give A Dog A Bone

Harry loped along beside his best buddy John, the grass of the park where John liked to go running soft beneath Harry's feet and the air rife with scents: clipped grass, John's sweat, pollen, and despite the bright sun overhead, humidity like just before a good rain.

Breathing easily through his mouth and letting his tongue loll out to cool himself, Harry was content to just follow along beside John until he heard something moving off to the left, away from the path of dark stone that John seemed to like so much.

A new scent came to his nostrils then, and his lips drew back over his teeth as he recognized it. Rabbit.

Letting out a little yip, Harry surged forward and to the left, anticipation of a nice little snack bringing saliva to his mouth and setting his tail to wagging.

Then the thing around his neck dug in, and he came up short. He reared in the air, fighting against the restraint, but to no avail. It held fast, as John willed it.

"Harry, come back here," John said.

Harry looked back to see John had stopped running and was looking at him with an expression that Harry had learned meant he disapproved of what Harry had done, but was not angry.

Loping back to his buddy, Harry closed the distance between them, only a couple strides, and looked up at him.

John squatted down, the blue and white second skins on his legs and torso bunching up as he did so. "What'd you see over here?" he said, though the words just came across as playful and companionable sounds, and little more. Far more important than the sounds, John reached out with both hands and scratched at the area behind Harry's ears.

Harry shivered in delight—he loved when John did that—and his tail got to wagging more fervently, of its own accord. Reaching up, he ran his tongue over the bottom half of John's face.

John leaned back and away, laughing, then straightened. He rubbed the top of Harry's head then said, "Come boy."

They ran some more, and Harry relished the feeling as his legs bunched and flexed and his toes dug into the dirt.

The stone path John followed continued through the field of grass and then passed beneath a cluster of weeping willows, though of course Harry didn't know the name for them. He always loved running beneath those tress because of the soft sound the dangling limbs and leaves made as they moved in the breeze, and because of the extensive shadow they cast. Harry wanted to just lie there and relax.

But John had other ideas, and the thing on Harry's neck urged him to keep up.

The willows were quickly forgotten, though, as

the path bent to the left and the scent of water grew more strongly on the breeze.

The lake.

Harry loved the lake.

He sped up, but again the thing on his neck held him back, keeping him close to John. But it was all Harry could do not to burst, his anticipation had him tingling so.

The path rounded a small rise, and there is was: the lake.

If he'd known the word, pond would have been a more appropriate term. The body of water was not particularly broad, nor was it deep. But it had the most wonderful something in the center that sent water spewing skyward and then falling back down in a mass of sparkles that shimmered and reflected the sunlight in glints and sometimes mini-rainbows.

As he always did, John stopped for a rest at a strange almost-forest that stood at the side of the lake. It was a bunch of trees that weren't trees, logs without limbs and leaves clustered together at weird angles, with dull grey hard tubes connecting some of them together in some places, but not in others.

As Harry and John approached, there was another person at the weird forest. A female from the shape and scent of her, in tight-fitting yellow and white second skins. She was hanging from one of the hard tubes between logs, her arms bent double as she trembled to hold her chin up above the tube.

Strange. But John seemed to like that she was doing it.

There was a wooden bench—Harry knew what that was—not far from the strange forest. John dropped the end of the thing on Harry's neck atop one of the cross-pieces that made up the bench's back, so it was loosely looped over one of them, then stepped over toward where the female was hanging.

He said something as she dropped back to the ground, and she turned to face him. Her lips pulled back from her teeth as she saw him, and despite Harry having lived with humans for so long, he had to restrain his fighting reflexes for a second.

Bared teeth meant different with them, he always had to remind himself.

Harry settled down onto his haunches while John and the female exchanged noises, but Harry's attempt at becoming comfortable was interrupted by a high-pitched "Oh…so cute," from the female.

And then he was having his ears scratched again, and Harry couldn't complain.

He flicked his tongue into the female's face and she laughed, then stepped away from Harry and turned back to John.

Harry sniffed, and caught a faint odor from her that he had last scented a few moons ago, when John had brought a different female to their house and the two of them had begun wrestling together on the couch. The odor of that female's arousal had been so overpowering Harry had had to flee to a different room.

This one's was not so pungent. But it was there, and one man to another, he felt happy for John.

Then a fly buzzed past Harry's face, its wings almost striking his snout. Annoyed, Harry nipped at the air, but missed the bug.

It came back, and Harry tried again.

And again, no luck.

Harry sniffed and turned away from the annoying insect, which anyway had flown off to bother someone else. He paused when something else new came to his nostrils.

The breeze had shifted so it was now blowing toward the lake, through the woods on the other side of the stone path from the not-trees on the shore. And there was something…

Harry started forward, and found himself surprised when the thing on his neck didn't restrain him. He looked back and saw that the end of it had fallen from the bench and was now dragging behind him; it must have come off when he was jumping after the fly.

Back by the not-trees, John and the female were still making noises at each other. John would be fine there, Harry was sure.

He could go find out what this new thing was.

Harry padded across the black stone and beneath the canopy of the woods. The grass that had lined the path quickly gave way to bare dirt, and Harry felt his toes dig more deeply into the cool, slightly moist soil. It was comforting, in a way.

The leaves overhead rustled, and somewhere off to the right a bird made a high-pitched call that Harry didn't know.

And the odor grew stronger.

It was strange. Like some of the meats that John liked to grill or broil, but fundamentally different in some way Harry couldn't put his nose on.

And rotten, of course. But that wasn't the strangeness; he had scented rotten before, and could pick out the various meats despite their rot, no problem.

But not this one.

He put his snout to the ground and ranged forward, moving left and right as he went further into the woods.

The scent was everywhere. But it seemed to be strongest coming from right…over…

Harry stopped in an area where the soil

seemed somehow softer than elsewhere. He sniffed; whatever that meat was, it was here.

Time to dig.

Harry lolled his tongue out, happiness washing over him. He loved to dig, too.

The soil *was* more loose here, and more damp as well. Little shivers of contentment flowed up Harry's legs as his toes dug into the moist coolness beneath, and loosed greater nose-fulls of the strangely enticing, yet also somehow abhorrent, odor beneath.

"Harry!"

His name—not his true name but the one John had given him—rang through the air, but Harry paid the call no heed. Faster he dug, his toes un-earthing hidden treasures that any other day he would have investigated for hours. Today, though, he only had nose for whatever it was that had cre-ated the odor that drew him on.

Deeper he went, and deeper still, and still it eluded him.

Another voice, higher-pitched, joined in with John's, calling out to him. "Harry!"

Part of Harry's mind grinned in triumph for his best buddy, for he had clearly secured himself a mate this day.

But that didn't matter, because what was causing that scent?

"There you are!" It was John's voice, near be-hind him.

And there it was. The last few pawfulls of dirt had unearthed it, and now it lay beneath him. It was decaying, but there was enough of it left to see it for what it was. It was rotting, but there was enough unturned meat to make its scent almost appealing.

Except that it resembled his best buddy so

much he would never dream of sinking his teeth into it.

"What is he getting into?" said the higher, female voice.

"No idea," said John, and then the thing on Harry's neck tightened, and strong arms pulled him back. "Come on, boy, get out of - "

John's voice broke, his sounds halting in a gurgle of surprise and shock.

The female made an, "Oh!" that was all fear mixed with revulsion.

John pulled Harry the rest of the way out of the hole Harry had made, and Harry only resisted a little bit. Because now he realized what it was he was looking at; an appendage just like his best buddy's, except it was detached from the body of the human who used to own it.

"Call 911," John said, and he swallowed hard.

The meaning of his sounds escaped Harry, but the sense of horror, of revulsion, with which he made them did not.

THE SUN WAS ALMOST GONE BEHIND the trees, and still they remained there in the not-forest of not-trees next to the lake.

Many more humans had come, strangely dressed in dark blue second-skins, with dark blue things atop their heads and a sense of officialness that implied a whole other skin that was invisible, but also undeniably there.

They had brought with them great noisy transports, like John's except larger, that had torn up the ground around the lake as they charged into the area and that flashed brilliant lights into the growing shadows of the fleeing day. White, Blue, and Red, they dazzled Harry's eyes every time he looked their way. So he stopped doing so, instead looking away from them toward the waters and the strangely comforting thing that spat upward in the center of the lake.

The official humans made noises at John again and again, and at his new mate. But eventually they let her go. She and John made noises to each other, and he did something with a flat black thing he always kept in a pouch of his second skin. Then she left, moving quickly past the flashing transports in the direction of a place Harry could vaguely recall.

Wasn't it in that direction that he and John had originally come from? Where John had left his own transport thing, so similar yet so much less disturbing than those that the official humans used?

Harry supposed it didn't really matter.

In the time—he had only a vague notion of time, just that things moved on from where they were, becoming something else but without notion of a goal to that becoming—Harry and John had waited there, other official humans, dressed less martially but possessing the same air of being about stern business, had cordoned off the woods where Harry had made his discovery.

Much to his disdain. Twice he had managed to loosen the thing on his neck and tried to go back there. And twice he had been intercepted and prevented from doing so.

Harry bared his teeth and growled at the last human who had stopped him and delivered him back to John, and the official human with him. How to make him understand Harry didn't want to eat the things under the trees?

He would never do that. Too much like his best buddy.

But he did want to know what they were, and how they got there.

It didn't matter; he never got the chance to look again. Not long after that second attempt, the official human with John clasped forearms with him, then turned his back on Harry's best buddy.

A breath later, John said, "Let's go, boy," and the thing on Harry's neck urged him into motion.

He walked next to John as John headed in the same direction the female had gone, some time earlier. Toward his transport, and then, Harry presumed, back home.

Drat it. If they went home he'd never be able to figure out -

He hadn't noticed until right this moment that in addition to the official humans, others had gathered around the lake. Humans of all shades, wearing all sorts of second skins, were watching the goings on with the official ones, and in the woods.

They smelled of curiosity and good humor. A few of dread. And one…

As he and John drew near to the one human who stood apart from the others, garbed in a single grey second skin, Harry's hackles rose.

The human's scent was mostly normal: sweat and the strange aromatic thing that they used to conceal their sweat. But beneath that, mostly emanating from the skin he had slung over his shoulder, came another scent that was both alluring and abhorrent.

A scent that Harry recognized from the woods over by the lake.

Harry bared his teeth and growled, and he surged forward toward the strange human.

"Harry - " John sounded surprised, and the thing on Harry's neck tightened for a second, then let go as Harry heard John fall behind him.

The strangely-scented human's eyes widened as Harry leapt onto him, and he collapsed onto the ground.

The skin that he had slung over his shoulder fell as well, landing on the ground a pace away.

Paying the human no further mind, Harry dove at the skin and began tearing at it.

"What the - ?"

"Help him!"

"Damn dog!"

"Harry!"

A multitude of voices rose from all around, but Harry paid them no heed. He bit at the skin, tearing at it… And then it opened, and its contents fell out.

Immediately, the mood among the surrounding humans shifted. From anger at Harry, they now smelled of revulsion, or horror.

Of anger.

And, from the one Harry had knocked over, of fear.

That human tried to scramble to his feet and run, but others surged forward and knocked him down.

"Don't move! You're under arrest!"

Official voices took over, but Harry only heard John's as he knelt down beside him.

"Easy boy," John said, but only the comforting tone carried meaning. "Come on."

The thing around his neck didn't need to pull him away from the skin on the ground. John's arms did that for him.

BACK AT HOME, and Harry raced ahead of John across the entryway and into his room, with its big couch and chairs, and his bed over in the corner.

He found his little round toy and leapt on it, biting and pressing down, then feeling a surge of supreme joy when it emitted its little high-pitched squeak.

Harry shook his head, thrashing the toy about, then tossed it aside and watched it bounce across the room.

Then he bounded forward to bite at it again.

Heard but unnoticed behind him, John was talking into his black thing as he followed Harry into the room.

" - must have been cutting his victims up and bringing the pieces to the park one by one."

A pause, which Harry barely registered as the toy's squeak rang out again. Then John shrugged.

"Cops told me sometimes these sickos like to hang around the crime scene. Gives them a feeling of power, to watch people's reaction to their work."

The toy bounced away, but Harry cast it from his mind. He had come near to his water bowl, and its odor reminded him of his need for drink.

He bent his head over and began lapping up the cool fluid.

"Yeah, I got her number. We're going out to-morrow night." John laughed. "We'll see. Later man."

Then he set the black thing down on the flat wooden thing that dominated the room.

Harry saw this from the corner of his eye but didn't pay any heed until John came over and squatted down next to him. He was carrying an-other skin in his hands.

"I've got something for you, boy," John said. Then his hands made some indecipherable move-ments with the skin he was holding.

A scent come straight from heaven issued forth as the skin opened, and Harry pulled his head up out of the water bowl. Was that - ?

It was.

John pulled a great big bone out of the skin. And not just a bone. It had meat on it.

Cow meat.

John held the bone out, and for a moment Harry could do nothing but just look at it, saliva flooding into his mouth as he took in the bounty before him.

Was this real?

"Come get it, boy," John said, and he wiggled the bone around in the air.

That was all the encouragement Harry needed. He thrust his head forward and closed his teeth around the proferred treat.

Cow meat and blood and salt and marrow and thousands other flavors at once struck Harry's tongue, and it was all he could do not to swoon on the spot. But he was made of sterner stuff than that.

Mostly.

Moving quickly lest he tempt fate into taking the bounty away, he hurried over to his bed, circled once, and lied down, bone and meat in front of him between his forepaws.

Then he began gnawing. And he did not intend to stop until every last bit of this tasty morsel was gone, though it take him a week.

He had no notion of what a week was; or even what a day or a year truly was. But what notion of time's passage he did have, he projected out to an equivalent length.

Or not. Whatever thought of time, or its mean-ing, fled before the flavors cascading through his tongue and into his body. He just chewed and chewed and chewed.

So captivated was he that he almost missed the comparatively small pleasure of John scratching him behind the ears and saying, "Good boy."

Almost.

Message From The Author

Thank you for reading my book. I hope you enjoyed reading it as much as I enjoyed writing it.

Every review helps an author out, so whether you loved this book, hated it, or something in between, please take a minute to tell other readers what you thought. All of the online retailers make it very easy to do, and I would really appreciate it.

Feel free to come say hi at my website or on Facebook. I always enjoy hearing from readers, especially since you all are, collectively, my boss.

I also have a weekly podcast, Story Time With Michael Kingswood, where I read stories and talk through some of the latest goings on in my world. I'd love to see you there.

Thanks again. My best to you and yours.

Warm Regards,
Michael Kingswood

Mailing List

If you enjoyed this book and would like word on new releases and special deals from Michael Kingswood, sign up for his newsletter on his website. Guaranteed to be spam-free, you can opt out at any time. And you can rest assured he will not share your information with anyone, for any reason.

https://michaelkingswood.com/newsletter-signup/

Michael Kingswood is 20-year veteran of the US Navy submarine force and a lifelong fan of science fiction and fantasy literature. His work has appeared in numerous collections and anthologies, to include the Fiction River Anthology series from WMG publishing. He holds a bachelors degree in Mechanical Engineering as well as a Master of Engineering Management and a Master of Business Administration. He has four children and currently resides in San Diego.

Find Michael Kingswood online at:

www.michaelkingswood.com

www.facebook.com/michael.kingswood

steemit.com/@michaelkingswood

The Champion

Veritas Morte

Story Collections

Tales Of Adventure #1

Tales Of Adventure #2

Short Story 10-Pack

A Jar Of Mixed Treats

Short Mystery 10-Pack

Short Fiction

Michael has also published a number of shorter works,
links to which can be found on his website.

www.ingramcontent.com/pod-product-compliance
Lightning Source LLC
Chambersburg PA
CBHW032054180726
48284CB00004B/1335